Hans Holbein, John Bewick, John Sidney Hawkins, Thomas
Hodgson

Emblems of Mortality

Representing, in upwards of fifty cuts, Death seizing all ranks and degrees

of people

Hans Holbein, John Bewick, John Sidney Hawkins, Thomas Hodgson

Emblems of Mortality
Representing, in upwards of fifty cuts, Death seizing all ranks and degrees of people

ISBN/EAN: 9783337191405

Printed in Europe, USA, Canada, Australia, Japan

Cover: Foto ©Andreas Hilbeck / pixelio.de

More available books at **www.hansebooks.com**

EMBLEMS

OF

MORTALITY;

REPRESENTING,

IN UPWARDS OF FIFTY CUTS,

DEATH

SEIZING ALL RANKS AND DEGREES
OF PEOPLE;

Imitated from a Painting in the Cemetery of the
Dominican Church at BASIL, in *Switzerland:*

With an APOSTROPHE to each, tranſlated from the
Latin and French.

Intended as well for the Information of the CURIOUS,
as the Inſtruction and Entertainment of YOUTH.

TO WHICH IS PREFIXED

A copious PREFACE, containing an hiſtorical Account
of the above, and other Paintings on this Subject,
now or lately exiſting in divers Parts of Europe.

LONDON:

Printed for T. HODGSON, in George's-Court,
St. John's-Lane, Clerkenwell.

MDCCLXXXIX.

PREFACE.

THE Work here prefented to the Reader is a Copy, with a fmall Variation noticed hereafter, as to the Cuts, and a Tranflation, as to the Letter Prefs, of one well known to the Curious by the Title of IMAGINES MORTIS, or *The Images of Death*; which is reported to be in reality indebted for its Exiftence to an Event that BOCCACE did but feign as the Occafion of writing his *Decameron*; I mean the Calamity of a Plague: And its Hiftory is as follows.

Pope EUGENIUS IV. having fummoned a Council to meet at the City of Bafle, or, as it is more ufually called, Bafil, in Switzerland; it accordingly met there in the Year 1431, and continued to fit for Seventeen Years, Nine Months, and Twenty-Seven Days, or, according to Mr. WALPOLE*, but Fifteen Years in the whole; and at this Council the Pope himfelf, and after his Death his Succeffor

* *Anecdotes of Painting*, 8vo. Vol. I. P. 12.

A   FELIX

FELIX V. SIGISMOND Emperor of Germany,
ALBERT II. then King of the Romans, and
many other Princes and Perfons of diftinguifhed
Rank were prefent. During the Sitting of this
Council, viz. in the Year 1439, the City of
Bafil was vifited with a Plague, which raged for
fome Time with extreme Violence, and carried
off many of the Nobility, and feveral Cardinals
and Prelates who attended that Council, fome of
whom were interred in the very Cemetery where
the Painting, of which we are about to fpeak,
now is; and, on the Ceffation of the Diftemper,
the furviving Members of the Council, with a
View to perpetuate the Memory of this Event,
and of their providential Deliverance from its
Effects, caufed to be painted in Oil on the Walls
of the Cemetery, near the Convent of the Do-
minicans, a *Dance of Death*, reprefenting all
Ranks of Perfons, from the Pope to the Pea-
fant, as individually feized by Death; adding
alfo to each Figure eight Lines in German,
four of them containing an Addrefs from Death
to them feverally, the other four their Reply.
The Name of the Painter employed on this Occafion has not been tranfmitted down to us with
Certainty; but fome Perfons have imagined that
this Painting was the Work of HANS HOLBEIN:
Whether it were done by him or another, fhall
be hereafter confidered; but, in the mean Time,

we

we shall here proceed to relate the subsequent History of the Painting itself.

It is, however, to be observed, that MATTHEW MERIAN, who, in 1649, published in German, at Franckfort, in small Quarto, a Book entitled TODTEN TANZ, or *Death's Dance*, containing Engravings from the above-mentioned Painting*, and from the Preface to whose Work, as translated into French, in an Edition printed at Basil in 1744, most of the foregoing Facts are extracted, does not speak in positive Terms as to the precise Time when the original Figures were painted, but only says, that they are believed, and with great Probability, to be of that Time in which he had placed them; in further Confirmation of which he has noticed, that SIGISMOND was

---

* As it may afford the Reader some Satisfaction to be informed particularly what Characters are represented in this Painting, we here give a List of them from MERIAN's Engravings mentioned in the Text: At the Beginning is a Cut of OECOLOMPADIUS preaching; next follows one of a Charnel-House, and two Figures of Death piping; after which, in distinct Cuts, are given the Pope, Emperor, Empress, King, Queen, Cardinal, Bishop, Duke, Duchess, Count, Abbot, Knight, Lawyer, Magistrate, Canon, Physician, Gentleman, Lady, Merchant, Abbess, Cripple, Hermit, Young Man, Usurer, Maiden, Musician, Herald, Mayor, Grand Provost, Buffoon, Pedlar, Blind Man, Jew, Pagan, Female Pagan, Cook, Peasant, Painter, Painter's Wife.

　himself

himſelf a Lover and extraordinary Patron of the Arts, and had always about him a Number of Artiſts ; and that JOHN AB EYCK, the Inventor of Oil Painting, flouriſhed in his Reign ; but Mr. WARTON * has related (though it does not appear on what Authority) not only that HOLBEIN was the Painter, but that the Subject in Queſtion was painted in 1543 ; in which I conceive him miſinformed : For MERIAN was, as he himſelf tells us, a Native of Baſil, and poſſibly might have had his Account by Tradition ; and, had the Painting been of no earlier a Date than 1543, it is hardly probable (conſidering too that it is in Oil) that it ſhould have been ſo much injured by Time as to ſtand in Need, as we find it did, of an almoſt total Repair in 1568 : To all which I add, that MERIAN ſeems ſo well ſatiſfied of the Truth of his Account, that he tells us further that the Figures were drawn from Nature, and are dreſſed each in the Habit of the Time ; and that thoſe of the Pope, Emperor, and King, are reſpectively Portraits of FELIX V. who ſucceeded EUGENIUS IV. SIGISMOND Emperor of Germany, and ALBERT II. King of the Romans ; all of whom, as we have before remarked, were preſent at the Council.

* *Hiſtory of Poetry*, Vol. II. P. 54, in a Note.

Mr.

Mr. WALPOLE* mentions that this Painting was repaired in 1529; but in this he seems to have been misled (accidentally taking one Date instead of another) by a Passage in the Preface to MERIAN's Book before cited. MERIAN informs us, that the Painting in Question having been much injured by Time, JOHN HUGH KLAUBER, a Painter, and Citizen of Basil, was, in 1568, employed to repair it; and that, finding a Vacancy on the Wall sufficient for his Purpose, he added at the Head of the Painting a Portrait of JOHANNES OECOLOMPADIUS, in Memory of the Reformation in 1529, to which his preaching the Gospel to all Ranks, as he did, might be supposed in some small Degree to contribute; and, at the End of the Painting, on another Part of the Wall, he added the Portraits of himself, his Wife, and his Children: And this Repair by KLAUBER, MERIAN tells us further, was commemorated in a Latin Tablet, which in his Time hung near the Painting. Some Time after, it was again repaired, and so, without any further Repair, it continued till MERIAN's Time; but KEYSLER, who visited it in 1729, in his *Travels*, Vol. I. P. 171, Edit. 8vo. 1760, relates, that the original Colours were then totally effaced, that only the Outlines of the Fi-

---

* *Anecdotes of Painting*, 8vo. Vol. I. P. 123.

gures

gures were left, and that it had then been lately repaired.

The Thought of this allegorical Reprefentation of Death, though in the prefent Inftance immediately fuggefted by the Event above related, was not in itfelf original, but borrowed in fome Meafure from a Kind of Mafquerade, which Mr. WARTON * obferves was anciently celebrated in the Churches abroad, particularly thofe of France (and, among others, it feems to have been performed in St. Innocent's Church at Paris) and in which all Ranks and Degrees of Perfons were perfonated by the Ecclefiaftics of thofe Churches, who all danced together, and then difappeared; and it is certain that before the Calamity abovementioned happened at Bafil, and confequently before this Painting there was begun, Allufions to a *Dance of Death* occurred in the Writings of the Authors of the Time, in Reference, no Doubt, to that Kind of Mafquerade. It were needlefs to introduce a Number of Quotations to fupport this Affertion; but as fome Proof may, perhaps, be expected, I here infert from *The Vifion of* PIERS PLOWMAN, written about 1350, the following Paffage, with which Mr. WARTON's *Hift. of Poetry*, Vol. II. P. 54, has furnifhed me:

* *Hiftory of Poetry*, Vol. I. P. 210.

" Death

" Death came driving after, and all to Duſt paſh'd
" Kings and Cæſars, Knights and Popes."

And I further find that, ſeveral Years prior to
the Breaking out of this Plague at Baſil, the Idea
had even been carried into Execution ; for that
in 1384, a *Death's Dance* had been painted at
Minden, in Weſtphalia* : But, no ſooner had
this Painting at Baſil been finiſhed, and become,
as it very ſoon after did, univerſally celebrated
all over Europe, but the *Dance of Death* became
a very favourite Subject, and was frequently
painted in public Buildings. The earlieſt In-
ſtance which has yet occurred, ſubſequent to the
Painting at Baſil, is one which Mr. WARTON +
mentions at Lubec, in the Portico of St. Mary's
Church, painted in 1463; and of which Dr.
NUGENT, in his *Travels*, Vol. I. P. 102, ſpeak-
ing of Lubec, gives the following Account :

" But the moſt noted Thing in St. Mary's
" Church is the Painting called *Death's Dance*, ſo
" much talked of in all Parts of Germany. It
" was originally drawn in 1463, but the Figures
" were repaired at different Times, as in 1588,
" 1642, and laſt of all in 1701. Here you ſee the
" Repreſentation of Death leading an Emperor
" in his imperial Robes, who with his other Hand

* WARTON's *Hiſt. of Poetry*, Vol. II. P. 54.   + Ibid.

" takes

" takes hold of such another Figure, which leads
" up a King; and so alternately a Figure of
" Death and a human Person through all Condi-
" tions and Stages of Life. The Intention of the
" Artist was to shew that Death pays no Regard to
" Age or Condition, which is more particularly
" expressed in the Verses underneath. They were
" composed at first in Plat Deutch, or Low Dutch;
" but at the last Repair, in 1701, it was thought
" proper to change them for German Verses,
" which were written by NATHANIEL SCHLOTT,
" of Dantzick." Of these Verses Dr. NUGENT has
inserted a Translation from the original German, by a Lady of Dantzick, from which it appears that the Originals consist of, first, an
Apostrophe of Death to all, and then an Address
of Death to one Individual; then follows his
Reply; after that, Death's Address to another;
next, his Reply; and so on. It further appears
from the Translation, that the Characters deli-
neated in the Painting are the following: The
Pope, Emperor, Empress, Cardinal, King, Bishop,
General, Abbé, Knight, Carthusian, Burgomaster,
Prebendary, Nobleman, Physician, Usurer, Chaplain, Steward, Church-Warden, Tradesman, Re-
cluse, Peasant, Young Man, Maiden, Infant,
Dancing-Master, and Fencing-Master.

In

In Addition to this Instance we learn, that, in the Reign of Henry the Sixth, one JENKEN CARPENTER caused to be painted at his Expence on the Walls of the Cloister of St. Paul's Cathedral, London*, the *Dance of* MACHABRAY, or *Dance of Death* †; and it is more than pro-

* Formerly called Pardon Church-Yard, about which, says WEEVER, *Ancient Funeral Monuments*, 4to Edition, 1767, P. 168, " was artificially and richly painted, the *Dance of* " *Death* commonly called the *Dance of Paul's*; the Picture " of Death leading all Estates."

The above JENKEN CARPENTER was Executor to Sir RICHARD WHITTINGTON, and had a Licence granted him, Anno 1430, 8 Hen. VI. to establish upon the Charnel-House of St. Paul's a Chaplain, to have eight Marks a Year.

WEEVER, *ubi supra.*

† STOW's *Survey of London*, Edit. 4to. 1618, P. 616. An Engraving of it is inserted in DUGDALE's *Hist. of St. Paul's*, Edit. 1658, P. 290, and under it are given LYDGATE's Verses, which he observes at the End he had translated,

" Not Word by Word, but following in Substance."

The Characters, as may be collected from the Titles to the Verses, are the Pope, Emperor, Cardinal, King, Patriarch, Constable, Archbishop, Baron, Princess, Bishop, Squire, Abbot, Abbess, Bailiff, Astronomer, Burgess, Canon Secular, Merchant, Chartreux, Serjeant, Monk, Usurer, Physician, Amorous Squire, Gentlewoman, Man of Law, Mr. JOHN REKILL Tregetour, [*i. e.* Jugler. See the Glossary to URRY's CHAUCER, Art. *Treget*] Parson, Juror, Minstrel, Labourer, Friar Minor, Child, Young Clerk, Hermit, the King eaten of Worms, MACHABREE the Doctor.——DUGDALE, P. 132, says that CARPENTER was a Citizen of London, and that the Painting at St. Paul's was in Imitation of that in the Cloister adjoining to St. Innocent's Church-Yard, in Paris.

bable

bable that the celebrated Painting of the same Kind in St. Innocent's Church, in Paris, in like Manner owes its Original to the Painting at Basil.

Nor are these the only Instances in which this Subject has been chosen for the Decoration of Buildings; for in 1525 it was painted at Annaberg, and in 1534, in the Castle or Palace at Dresden; as it also was, though when is unknown, at Leipsic and other Places *.

The same Inclination in Favour of this Subject began also, very soon after the Painting in Question was known, to discover itself in literary Publications, and in the Decorations and Ornaments of Books. One MACABER, a French or German Poet, but of what Æra is uncertain, wrote in German a Poem on the Subject of *Death's Dance*, which, in Consequence of this Circumstance, is not seldom from him called *The Dance of* MACABER †.

His

---

* WARTON's *History of Poetry*, Vol. II. P. 54.

† Mr. WARTON, in his *Observations on* SPENSER, first Edit. P. 230, in a Note, says, that MACABER wrote a Description in Verse of a Procession, painted on the Walls of St. Innocent's Cloister, at Paris, called the *Dance of Death*; so that in this Passage Mr. WARTON must be supposed to understand that MACABER's Verses were written posterior to that Painting. He further informs us, in the Additions and Corrections to the

second

His Verſes were tranſlated into French, and written round the Cloiſter of St. Innocent's, at Paris, under, as I conceive, the before-mentioned Painting; and from this French Tranſlation, LYDGATE, at the Requeſt of the Dean and Chapter of St. Paul's *, made a Verſion, which was afterwards inſcribed on the Walls of their Church, under the Painting of the ſame Subject.

ſecond Volume of his *Hiſtory of Poetry*, that the earlieſt complete French Tranſlation of theſe Verſes was printed in 1499, but that a leſs perfect Edition had been before publiſhed in 1486, and that the French Rhymes in this laſt are ſaid to be by MICHEL MAROT. A Copy in French of *La grande Danſe de* MACABRE *des Hommes et des Femmes*, printed in 4to. at Troyes, for JOHN GARNIER, but without a Date, I have ſeen; and find from the Verſes under each Cut, that the Characters are the Pope, Emperor, Cardinal, King, Legate, Duke, Patriarch, Conſtable, Archbiſhop, Knight, Biſhop, Squire, Abbot, Bailiff, Aſtrologer, Burgeſs, Canon, Merchant, School-Maſter, Man of Arms, Chartreux, Serjeant, Monk, Uſurer, Phyſician, Lover, Advocate, Minſtrel, Curate, Labourer, Proctor, Gaoler, Pilgrim, Shepherd, Cordelier, Child, Clerk, Hermit, Adventurer, Fool. The Women are the Queen, Ducheſs, Regent's Wife, Knight's Wife, Abbeſs, Squire's Wife, Shepherdeſs, Cripple, Burgeſs's Wife, Widow, Merchant's Wife, Bailiff's Wife, Young Wife, Dainty Dame, Female Philoſopher, New-married Wife, Woman with Child, Old Maid, Female Cordelier, Chambermaid, Intelligence-Woman, Hoſteſs, Nurſe, Prioreſs, Damſel, Country Girl, Old Chambermaid, Huckſtreſs, Strumpet, Nurſe for Lying-in Women, Young Girl, Religious, Sorcereſs, Bigot, Fool.

* WARTON's *Hiſt. of Poetry*, Vol. II. P. 53.

It

It would be an endlefs Tafk, and afford but little Entertainment to the Reader, to reckon up here a long Lift of Books in which the Subject has been reiterated : We fhall therefore content ourfelves with mentioning that it appeared in the Chronicle of HARTMANNUS SCHEDELIUS, printed at Nuremberg in 1493, Folio*, ufually called the Nuremberg Chronicle; in the Quotidian Offices of the Church, printed at Paris, 1515, in 8vo †; in feveral Horæ, Miffals, &c. and even fo late as in *A Book of Chriftian Prayers, collected out of the ancient Writers and beft learned of our Time*, firft printed in 4to. 1569, and afterwards in the fame Size in 1608 ; and that, in Addition to all thefe and others which might be mentioned, the Painting at Bafil was the Caufe of the Publication of the IMAGINES MORTIS, from which the prefent is copied and tranflated, and of which therefore it will be neceffary here to give an Account; firft obferving, that the Excellence of the Cuts in the Original, which are here alfo copied with fufficient Fidelity, has induced an Opinion that they were the Work of HOLBEIN, a Fact which we mean hereafter to inquire into.

PAPILLON, in his *Traité hiftorique et pratique de la Gravure en Bois*, 8vo. 1766, Tom. I. F. 166,

* WARTON's *Hiftory of Poetry*, Vol. II. P. 54.   † Ibid.

informs

informs us, that HOLBEIN, having arrived to a great Degree of Perfection in Painting, was employed by a Magistrate of Basil to paint a *Dance of Death* in the Fish-Market of that City, near a Cemetery (by which he undoubtedly means the Painting at Basil, of which we have so often had Occasion to speak); that this Work added much to his Reputation; after which he employed his Skill in reducing the original Figures into a small Size; and that he afterwards engraved them upon Wood, with a Delicacy and Beauty not to be equalled. But unfortunately PAPILLON here speaks without sufficient Attention; for the Painting at Basil, as may be learnt from MERIAN's Engravings before mentioned, and on the Accuracy of which I am assured by an ingenious Friend, who lately examined them with the Originals, I may rely, consists of single Figures, each led by a Figure of Death, and following each other in order, so as to form a long Procession: The same may be remarked of the Painting at St. PAUL's; and, for aught that appears to the contrary, of that at Lubec, and of that at St. Innocent's Church at Paris, and probably of all the others which we have noticed above: Whereas the present Cuts consist of separate Compartments, each containing Groupes of Figures, so that the present Work is by no means merely a Reduction in Size of the Painting at Basil, but is rather to be considered as founded on

the

the fame Idea, and fuggested by the Original, than as a Copy from it.

The earliest Edition of the IMAGINES MOR-TIS which I have as yet feen, is one printed, as appears from the Colophon at the End, by MEL-CHIOR and GASPAR TRECHSEL, in fmall 4to. at Lyons, in 1538: It is in French, and its Title is as follows: " *Les Simulachres & Hiftoriees* " *faces de la Mort, autant elegamment pourtraictes,* " *que artificiellement imaginees: A Lyons, foulz l' Efcu* " *de Cologne.*" But PAPILLON, *in Loco fupra cit,* tells us, that the Cuts to the IMAGINES MORTIS must have been done about the Year 1530, for that the four first of them occur among HOLBEIN's Cuts to the Old Teftament, printed in 1539; and that it is apparent from thofe among the Scripture Cuts, that the Blocks had then already furnifhed many Thoufands of Impreffions. That the four first Cuts of the IMAGINES MORTIS are among the Scripture Cuts of HOLBEIN, is certainly true; but I think I once faw, in the Hands of a Friend, a Copy of the vulgate Latin Bible, in which thofe Scripture Cuts were in-ferted, and which, if my Memory does not greatly deceive me, was printed fo early as in or about 1518 or 1520.

The fame Author further relates, that the first Edition, which he thinks for the above Reafons
fhould

should be placed in the Year 1530, was printed at Bafil, or Zuric, with a Title to each Cut, and, as he believes, fome Verfes under each, all in the German Language (but, that there was an early Edition in Flemifh); and adds, that the Book, having paffed over into France, was much fought after by the Curious there; fo that a Printer of Lyons was induced to purchafe the Blocks, and that from them he printed feveral Editions in Latin, French, and Italian.

Having thus accounted for the Exiftence of the Book, and for its Arrival in France, it remains to fpeak of the feveral Impreffions which it there underwent. We have already mentioned one, the earlieft which we know of, printed in fmall Quarto, at Lyons, *foulz l'Efcu de Cologne*, by MELCHIOR and GASPAR TRECH-SEL, in 1538: The Cuts in this Edition are forty-three in Number, and no more; and over each is, in Latin, a Paffage from either the Old or New Teftament or Apocrypha, which, in the prefent Publication, is given in Englifh, from the Tranflation of the Bible now in ufe. Under the Cuts are four Lines in French Verfe, the Subftance of which has been preferved in all the Editions, whether they were in Latin, French, or Italian. This Edition, in order to make it of a tolerable Size (for the Cuts alone would have been too few to conftitute a Volume) is accom-

panied

panied with several Tracts in French, which, as
not relating to, or connected with, our present Subject, we here forbear to enumerate; but it is ne-
cessary, before we close our Account of this Edition of 1538, to remark, that it is preceded by a Dedication in French, to the very Reverend Abbess of
the Religious Convent of St. PETER of Lyons, Ma-
dam JEHANNE DE TOUSZELE; and in this Dedication the Author of it notices, that the Name
and Surname (or, as we term them, the Christian
and Surname) of the Abbess and himself are
precisely the same in sound, excepting only the
Letter T, from which I conjecture (for his Name
does not any where appear) that his Name was
JEAN, or, as it was anciently written, JEHAN
[i. e. JOHN] DE OUSZELL, or OZELL, as
it is now usually spelt. In this Dedication is
also a Passage, a Translation of which will be
given hereafter, from which it appears that the
Person by whom the Cuts were designed, was
then dead, leaving behind him several others of
the same Kind, which, though drawn, were
unfinished, and particularly one representing a
Waggoner crushed under his overthrown Waggon; in which Cut, a Figure of Death is represented secretly sucking through a Reed, the
Wine out of a Cask; and that to these unfinished
Cuts no one had dared to put the last Hand.

The next Edition, in Point of Time, which I
have

have feen, I conceive to have been the firft that
appeared in Latin, and it was printed in Duo-
decimo, at Lyons, *fub fcuto Colonienfi*, by JOHN
and FRANCIS FRELLON, in 1542. It contains
the fame Number of Cuts (and no more) as that
of 1538, and is entitled, " *Imagines de Morte, et*
" *Epigrammata e Gallico idiomate a Georgio Æmylio*
" *in Latinum tranflata;*" from whence it appears
that it is, in Fact, a Tranflation of the French
Edition of 1538. This alfo contains fome additional Tracts, all differing from thofe in the
Edition of 1538, but not in the leaft relating to
the prefent Inquiry, and therefore not here par-
ticularized, though they have been continued
through almoft all the fubfequent Impreffions,
and have been given refpectively in French, Latin, and Italian, according as the Verfes under
the Cuts to the IMAGINES MORTIS were in one
or other of thofe Languages.

In 1547, another Edition was publifhed of
this Book, in French; it was entitled, " *Les*
" *Images de la Mort,*" and printed at Lyons, *A
l'Efcu de Cologne, Chez* JEHAN FRELLON; the
Title-Page alfo informs us that twelve Cuts are
added to it, and on Examination we find that the
Cuts inferted in Page 40, and the feven fubfequent Pages of this Work, and four Cuts of
Boys, which, as not relating to this Subject, are in
the prefent Edition omitted (none of which occur

in

in either the French Edition of 1538, or the Latin one of 1542, the only two prior Editions that I know of) are to be found in this of 1547 *.

In the fame Year, viz. 1547, but whether prior or fubfequent to the laft above mentioned, cannot be known, another Latin Edition appeared, printed at Lyons by the fame JOHN FRELLON, and containing the fame increafed Number of Cuts as the French one of the fame Year, that is to fay, fifty-three in all; and the fame JOHN FRELLON, in 1549, printed an Edition of this Work in Italian and Latin, the Paffages from Scripture over the Cuts being in Latin, and the Verfes under the Cuts in Italian; and this alfo contains the fame Number of Cuts with the two laft-mentioned Editions: But PAPILLON, P. 169, remarks that the Blocks, when this Edition of 1549 was printed, had already furnifhed more than an hundred-thoufand Impreffions, for that in fome Places they appear to be worn.

In 1562, the fame JOHN FRELLON publifhed another French Edition, which appears, by the Printer's Colophon at the End, to have been printed at Lyons by SYMPHORIEN BARBIER, and which profeffes in the Title to be augmented

* It cannot be doubted that thefe additional Cuts are thofe mentioned in the Dedication to the Edition of 1538, as being then left unfinifhed, for, among them, is the Cut of the Waggoner there particularly defcribed.

with

with feventeen Plates. PAPILLON, P. 182, mentions both this Edition and Peculiarity, but denies the Truth of the Affertion, becaufe he tells us, that in this French Edition he finds but five more Cuts than in the Italian One of 1549; notwithftanding which, it is certainly true, as will be prefently proved. PAPILLON admits that the Edition of 1562 contains five Cuts more than that of 1549, and, if he had gone farther back in his Refearch, would have found that that of 1549 (and fo do the French and Latin Editions of 1547) comprizes twelve more than that of 1538, and that thofe twelve were firft added to the French and Latin Editions of 1547. The Edition of 1562 does not affert that that contains feventeen Cuts more than any preceding Edition, but, reckoning the five which it has more than the Impreffion of 1549, and the twelve which that has more than the Edition of 1538, and which are alfo inferted in that of 1562, they make together feventeen Cuts more than were in the Edition of 1538, and confequently juftify the Affertion in the Title, that the Edition of 1562 contains feventeen additional Cuts.

The Succefs which fuch a Number of Editions feems to imply, induced a Bookfeller of Cologne to counterfeit the Book; and, inftead of making ufe of the original Cuts, which, in all Probability he could not procure, he got Copies,

2

and not very exact ones, engraven from them
for his intended Edition. When the firft coun-
terfeited Edition appeared, I am not informed;
but am induced to think that this Perfon, whom
I have above defcribed as a Bookfeller of Cologne, was ARNOLD BIRCKMAN, as I find an
Edition, printed in 1555, at Cologne, *Apud hæ-
redes* ARNOLDI BIRCKMANNI. In this Edition,
and alfo in one printed by the fame Perfons in
1573, the Cuts are reverfed, the Paffages from
Scripture over the Cuts, and alfo the Verfes under
the Cuts, are in Latin; and both thefe Editions
contain the Number of Cuts in the Latin and
French ones of 1547, and no more: In the Cut
inferted P. 17, of the prefent Edition, is the following Mark *Æ* (intended, no doubt, for that
of the Engraver) and which was that of SILVIUS
ANTONIANUS, an Artift of confiderable Merit.

Having thus given the Hiftory of this celebrated Work, we are now to inquire, in the firft
Place, whether the original Painting at Bafil
were, or not, painted by HOLBEIN; and, in the
fecond, whether the IMAGINES MORTIS were
either defigned or engraven by him.

As to the firft of thefe Queftions it is to be
obferved, that MERIAN, whom we have above
mentioned, has related that this Picture at Bafil
was painted during the fitting of the Council
before

before mentioned, which met in 1431, and fat either fifteen, according to fome, or fomething more than feventeen Years, according to other Authors; fo that the Painting now under Confideration muft have been done between the Years 1439, when the Plague broke out, and 1446, or 1448, when the Council broke up; now it is certain that HOLBEIN was not born till 1498*: nor do we find that he was ever employed on the Painting at Bafil, even fo much as to re-touch it. HUGH KLAUBER, who repaired it in 1568, is recorded, and it is not probable that, if it ever had been touched upon by HOLBEIN, that Fact fhould, in his own native City, have been paffed over in Silence: On the contrary, it is more likely that an Opportunity fhould have been rather fought to reveal it†.

From thefe Confiderations it appears pretty evidently, that HOLBEIN has no Claim to the Painting at Bafil: We now proceed, therefore, to the fecond Inquiry, viz. Whether he either defigned or engraved the original Cuts to the IMAGINES MORTIS, and here it may firft be neceffary to ftate what Reafons there may be for fuppofing them his.

NICOLAS

* WALPOLE's *Anecdotes of Painting*, Vol. I. P. 123.

† KEYSLER, in his Travels before referred to, Vol. I. P. 171, fpeaking of the *Dance of Death*, at Bafil, fays, it is gene-rally reputed to have been painted by HOLBEIN, who had

alfo

NICOLAS BORBONIUS, a Poet contemporary with HOLBEIN, has addreſſed to him an Epigram " *De Morte piɛta, a Hanſo Piɛtore nobili**," from which it is inferred that he painted a *Dance of Death*; and SANDRART relates that in the Year 1627, in a Converſation with RUBENS, at which he was preſent, the IMAGINES MORTIS was ſtiled HOLBEIN's, as will appear from the following Paſſage, tranſlated by Mr. WARTON from JOACH. SANDRART, *Academ. Piɛt.* Part II. Lib. iii. Cap. 7. P. 241, " I alſo well remember " that in the Year 1627, when PAUL RUBENS " came to Utrecht to viſit HANDORST, being " eſcorted both coming from, and returning to " Amſterdam, by ſeveral Artiſts; as we were in " the Boat, the Converſation fell upon HOL- " BEIN's Book of Cuts repreſenting the *Dance* " *of Death*, that RUBENS gave them the higheſt " Encomiums, adviſing me, who was then a " young Man, to ſet the higheſt Value upon " them; informing me, at the ſame Time, that " he, in his Youth, had copied them." WAR- TON's *Obſervations on* SPENSER, firſt Edit. P.

alſo drawn and painted a *Death's Dance*, and had likewiſe painted, as it were, a Duplicate of this Piece on another Houſe, but which Time has entirely obliterated. " However," adds he, " for ſeveral Reaſons the *Death's Dance* near the " French Church may be preſumed not to be HOLBEIN's, " but the Work of another Artiſt whoſe Name was BOCK."

* WARTON's *Obſervations on* SPENSER, Vol. II. P. 117, in the Note.

231, in a Note, where is also inserted a Translation from the same Work, P. 238, in the following Words, " But, in the Fish-Market there"
[at Basil] " may be seen his" [HOLBEIN's]
" admirable *Dance of Peasants*, where also, in
" the same public Manner, is shewn his *Dance*
" *of Death* ; where, by a Variety of Figures, it is
" demonstrated that Death spares neither Popes,
" Emperors, Princes, &c. as may be seen in his
" most elegant wooden Cuts of the same Work."

In BULLART's *Academie des Sciences*, Tom. II.
P. 412, is a Passage, of which the following is a
Translation : " Neverthelefs, he" [HOLBEIN]
" has not sent any Thing into the World which is
" not painted with the last Degree of Perfection.
" The Inhabitants of Basil have an excellent Wit-
" nefs of this in their Town-Houfe : It is his Piece
" of the *Dance of Death*, which he has reduced
" into Colours, after having engraven them
" very neatly on Wood; and which appeared fo
" excellent to the learned ERASMUS, that,
" after having publifhed his Praifes, he invited
" HOLBEIN to draw his Picture, in order that
" he might have the Happinefs of being repre-
" fented by fo fkilful a Hand."

Monf. PATIN, in the Catalogue of HOL-
BEIN's Works, prefixed to his Edition of ERAS-
MUS's *Praife of Folly*, in Latin, clofes his Lift
with

with Words to the following Effect, " He also
" engraved feveral Things upon Wood, among
" which are his *Scripture Cuts*, and *Dance of*
" *Death*, vulgarly called *Toden Tans*; from which
" that Picture is not very different, which was
" painted from the Life by the Hand, as fome
" think, of HOLBEIN himfelf, and is enclofed
" by wooden Pallifadoes from Strangers in the
" Cemetery of the Predicants, in the Suburbs of
" St. JOHN, at Bafil:" And PRIOR takes it for
fo acknowledged a Fact that HOLBEIN painted
the well-known *Dance of Death*, that, in his
Ode to the Memory of Colonel GEORGE VILLIERS,
he thus alludes to it:

" In vain we think that free-will'd Man has Pow'r
" To haften or protract th' appointed Hour.
" Our Term of Life depends not on our Deed;
" Before our Birth, our Fun'ral was decreed.
" Nor aw'd by Forefight, nor mifled by Chance,
" Imperious Death directs the Ebon Lance,
" Peoples great HENRY's Tombs, and leads up
      HOLBEIN's Dance."

By " great HENRY's Tombs," HENRY the Se-
venth's Chapel in Weftminfter-Abbey is meant.

To refute by minute Examination the feveral
Errors in the above Citations, would be an almoft
endlefs Tafk; it is fufficient here to remark, that
the Paffage from BORBONIUS is too general to
                                    afcertain

ascertain, whether he means a *Dance of Death*, or a single Figure; that SANDRART or RUBENS's Declaration is too far distant from the Time, to be of any great Weight; as is also PATIN's Assertion, that HOLBEIN actually engraved the IMAGINES MORTIS: And surely, if it had been either designed or engraven by him, FRELLON, for whom so many Editions were printed, would not have failed to have mentioned it in some of them, when we find, that in the Editions of the *Scripture Cuts*, which he printed, he has inserted a Latin Poem of some Length, and also a Greek Epigram, both by BORBONIUS, with a Translation of this latter into Latin, all to prove, that the Cuts were the Work of HOLBEIN. It is further to be observed (as one Reason for ascribing these Cuts to HOLBEIN) that a Cut of the IMAGINES MORTIS, which occurs P. 36 of this Edition, but the Mark is there purposely omitted, has to it in the original the Letters H L thus conjoined HL which PAPILLON asserts, is one of the Marks of HOLBEIN; and CHRISTIAN DE MECHEL, Engraver to the Elector Palatine, seems so well convinced of their being really at least designed by HOLBEIN, that he has inserted the *Dance of Death*, as represented in the IMAGINES MORTIS, among the rest of his Works, which he is now publishing; but the Number of Cuts there given, is no more than Forty-Six.

It were much to be wished that MECHEL had
b   informed

informed us, from what he had copied the *Dance of Death;* whether, as he probably did, from Drawings; and, if so, where those Drawings were to be found, and on what further Evidence he had ventured to ascribe them to HOLBEIN; for, as will presently appear, there is very great Reason, at least, for doubting the Fact, notwithstanding that the four first Cuts of the IMAGINES MORTIS occur among the Cuts to the Old Testament, printed in 1539, and which we are told expressly in a Poem, and also in an Epigram, of BORBONIUS, prefixed to them, are of the Hand of HOLBEIN; but whether by this we are to understand, that he designed or engraved them, or both, we are left to seek. After having thus ventured to question in general Terms, HOLBEIN's Title to the Merit of this Work, it is incumbent on me to shew on what my Doubts are founded, and this I am prepared to do; for, in the Dedication to the Edition of the IMAGINES MORTIS, in 1538, is a Passage, of which I here insert a faithful Translation:

      € "To return then to our *Cuts of Death,* we
" now very justly regret the Death of him
" who has here designed such elegant Figures,
" exceeding as much all the Examples hitherto,
" as the Paintings of APELLES, or of ZEUXIS,
" exceed the Moderns. For his sorrowful His-
" tories, with their Descriptions severely versi-
" fied, excite such Admiration in the Beholders,
                         " that

" that they think the Figures of Death appear
" as if quite alive, and the Living as if dead.
" Which makes me think that Death, fearing
" that this excellent Painter would paint him so
" much alive, that he fhould no longer be feared
" as Death, and that, for this Reafon, he him-
" felf would become immortal; for this very
" Caufe haftened fo much his Days, that he
" could not finifh feveral other Cuts already by
" him traced, and among others that of the
" Waggoner overthrown and bruifed under his
" overturned Waggon; the Wheels and Horfes
" of which are there reprefented fo frightfully,
" that as much Horror is occafioned to view
" their Downfall, as Delight to contemplate the
" Liquorifhnefs of one Figure of Death, who is
" fecretly fucking through a Reed the Wine
" from the emptied Cafk : To which imperfect
" Hiftories, as well as to the inimitable Rainbow,
" no one has dared to put the laft Hand."

This Dedication is prefixed to the Edition of
1538, and fpeaks of the Defigner (by which, I
conceive, we muft underftand both Painter and
Engraver, for it fpeaks of the Drawings of the
unfinifhed ones as having been then already
traced or drawn; and, if fo, they might furely
have been finifhed by the Engraver of the former
ones) as then lately dead; now it is well known
that HOLBEIN did not die till! 1554*, and there-

* WALPOLE'S *Anecdotes of Painting*, Vol. I, P. 115.

fore it could not be he : And I would further ob-
ferve, that the Mark H̶L̶ is not peculiar to HoL-
BEIN. STRUTT, in his *Biographical Dictionary
of Engravers*, Vol. II. P. 86, attributes it to
one HANS LEDERER, of whom he gives no
Particulars ; and the *Catalogue of Marks and Cy-
phers of Engravers*, P. 21. Edit. 1730, mentions
one LAMBRECHT HOPFER, a German, but the
Age in which he lived is not noticed, who
ufed, as his Mark, fometimes a Vafe of Flowers
in the Midft of the Letters L H, and fometimes
the perpendicular Stroke of the L in the fecond
Stroke of the H, which is exactly as it appears
in the Cut before referred to.

I have only to add, that the Cuts in the prefent Edition, excepting only the firft (which,
reprefenting in the Original the Deity in the
Habit of the Pope, to avoid giving Offence, it was
thought proper to omit, and to fubftitute in its
Room one defigned for the Purpofe) are engraven, and the Verfes under them tranflated,
from the Latin Edition of 1547 ; and that the additional Cuts, which appeared in the French Edition of 1562 (with the Omiffion only of four of
Boys, as being foreign to this Subject) are here
alfo inferted, and the Verfes under them tranflated
from the French.

THE EDITOR.

March 24, 1789.

The CREATION of the WORLD.

So God created Man in his own Image, in the
Image of God created he him: Male and Female
created he them.

GENESIS i. 27.

In the Beginning, Heav'n and Earth,
  And the refounding Sea,
God, by his Voice omnipotent,
  From Nothing caus'd to be.

The human Race, the Image true
  Of his divineft Mind,
Both Male and Female he did form
  From lighteft Earth we find.

B

S I N.

Becauſe thou haſt hearkened unto the Voice of thy
Wife, and haſt eaten of the Tree of which I com-
manded thee, ſaying, Thou ſhalt not eat of it, &c.

GENESIS iii. 17.

Againſt God's Will the direful Fruit
  Of the forbidden Tree
The Huſband by his fooliſh Wife
  To taſte induc'd we ſee.

A grievous Death they both deſerv'd
  For this Offence ſo great,
And we, their Children, ſubject are
  To the ſame Laws of Fate.

3

DEATH.

The Lord God ſent him forth from the Garden of Eden to till the Ground, from whence he was taken.

GENESIS iii. 23.

Th' Almighty Father did expel
  Man from his bleſſed Seat;
And to ſuſtain his Life decreed
  By his own proper Sweat:

Then, firſt, into the empty World,
  Pale Death an Entrance gain'd;
And the ſame Pow'r o'er mortal Men,
  Has ever ſince maintain'd.

The CURSE.

Cursed is the Ground for thy Sake; in Sorrow shalt thou eat of it all the Days of thy Life, &c.

GENESIS iii. 17.

Curs'd be the Earth for thy Offence,
   And barren be the Ground,
And full of Toil and Labour great,
   Thy anxious Life be found;

Till Death thy lifeless Limbs replace
   In Earth's cold narrow Womb,
Then Dust, which at the first thou wert,
   Thou quickly shalt become.

Woe, Woe, Woe to the Inhabiters of the Earth.
REVELATIONS viii. 13.

All in whose Noſtrils was the Breath of Life, of all that was in the dry Land, died.
GENESIS vii. 22.

Woe, grievous Woe, to all who now
 In this vile World abide;
For Times await you big with Grief,
 And every Ill beſide.

Though now to you a plenteous Share
 Of Fortune's Gifts may fall,
Pale Death will be, or ſoon or late,
 A Viſitant to all.

The POPE.

Until the Death of the High-Prieſt that ſhall be in thoſe Days. JOSHUA xx. 6.

And let another take his Office. PSALM cix. 8.

Thou who, elated with Succeſs,
   Immortal claim'ſt to be,
From Men's Affairs, in little Space,
   Thyſelf remov'd ſhalt ſee.

Though now the great High-Prieſt thou art,
   And in Rome's See doſt ſit,
Soon ſhall thy Office, in thy Place,
   A Succeſſor admit.

The EMPEROR.

*Set thine House in Order; for thou shalt die, and
not live.* ISAIAH XXXVIII. 1.

*There shalt thou die, and there the Chariots of thy
Glory shall be the Shame of thy Lord's House.*
ISAIAH XXII. 18.

Dispose thy Kingdom's great Concerns
   Intrusted to thy Care,
So that to pass to other Worlds
   Thou quickly may'st prepare.

For when the Time shall come that thou
   Shalt quit this mortal Throne,
Thy utmost Glory then shall be
   A broken Car alone.

The KING.

He that is To-Day a King To-Morrow shall die.

ECCLESIASTICUS X. 10.

To him who this Day Sceptres sways,
   In costly Pride a King,
To-Morrow's Light, with baleful Speed,
   A direful Fate will bring :

For, him who rules o'er Nations rich,
   And pow'rful Kingdoms guides,
When Death his Office bids him quit,
   No better Fate betides.

The CARDINAL.

Which justify the Wicked for Reward, and take away the Righteousness of the Righteous from him.

ISAIAH V. 23.

Woe, grievous Woe, to you, who now
 The impious Man carefs ;
Exalt the unjuft to Height of Wealth,
 The virtuous Man opprefs.

Who feek the World's fallacious Gifts
 To gain without Delay,
And the true Path of Righteoufnefs
 Defire to take away.

The EMPRESS.

Thofe that walk in Pride he is able to abafe.

DANIEL iv. 37.

Ye, alfo, who in glitt'ring Pomp
   Of haughty State are plac'd,
A Day fhall fee wherein yourfelves
   Of bitter Death fhall tafte :

For, as the Grafs by Travellers
   Is trodden on the Ground,
So Death fhall tread you under Foot,
   And all your Joys confound.

The QUEEN.

Rise up, ye Women that are at Ease; hear my Voice,
ye careless Daughters; give Ear unto my Speech.
Many Days and Years shall ye be troubled.

ISAIAH xxxii. 9 & 10.

Hither, ye Ladies of Renown,
   And Matrons rich, repair;
For Death to you now clearly tells,
   A mortal Tribe ye are.

When the glad Years and empty Joys
   Of this vain World are past,
The Pain of Death will sure disturb
   Your Bodies frail at last.

The BISHOP.

*I will smite the Shepherd, and the Sheep of the
Flock shall be scattered abroad.*

MATTHEW xxvi. 31. MARK xiv. 27.

The Pastor, void of all Defence,
· My Pow'r, says Death, shall own;
By me, his Mitre and his Staff,
Shall to the Ground be thrown.

His Sheep, their Pastor thus remov'd,
By Death's fell Pow'r, away,
Shall be dispersed ev'ry one,
To prowling Wolves a Prey.

The ELECTOR, or PRINCE of the Empire.

The Prince shall be clothed with Desolation, and the Hands of the People of the Land shall be troubled.

EZEKIEL vii. 27.

Come, mighty Prince, now quick resign
    Thy perishable Joys,
Thy fleeting Glory, and the rest
    Of Earth's delusive Toys.

Lo, I alone the Pride of Kings
    Am able to repress;
The splendid Pomps of regal State
    My Pow'r supreme confess.

C

The ABBOT.

*He shall die without Instruction, and in the Greatness
of his Folly he shall go astray.*

PROVERBS V. 23.

This Instant, Wretch, thou shalt depart,
　Consign'd to mould'ring Dust ;
Because thou knew'st not, only feign'dst,
　The Wisdom of the Just.

The Abundance of thy Folly great,
　Did blindly thee deceive,
And made thee seek the sinful Path,
　Which thou could'st never leave.

The ABBESS.

Wherefore I praised the Dead which are already dead,
more than the Living which are yet alive.

ECCLESIASTES iv. 2.

Better it is to die than live,
   I conſtantly have taught ;
Since human Life with anxious Care,
   And various Ills is fraught.

Ungrateful Death me now compels
   The like ſad Path to tread,
With thoſe whom in the ſilent Grave
   The Fates ſevere have laid.

C 2

The GENTLEMAN.

What Man is he that liveth, and shall not see Death?
Shall he deliver his Soul from the Hand of the Grave?

PSALM lxxxix. 48.

What Man is he, however brave,
  Of mightiest Pow'r possest,
Who in this mortal World shall live,
  And Death shall never taste?

What Man is he who Death's fell Dart,
  Which conquers all, can brave?
Who his own Life, by Force or Skill,
  From Death can hope to save?

The CANON.

Behold, the Hour is at Hand.

MATTHEW xxvi. 45.

By Crowds attended to the Choir
   Thou now doſt bend thy Way;
Come on, and, with ſuppliant Voice,
   Thy humbleſt Homage pay:

For, thee the Fates do loud demand,
   And inſtant Death does crave;
A Day, which no one can retard.
   Shall force thee to the Grave.

The J U D G E.

I will cut off the Judge from the Midst thereof.

Amos ii. 3.

You who falfe Judgment do pronounce,
  For filthy Lucre's Sake,
From Midſt of Crowds and Judgment-Seat,
  I, Death, will quickly take.

To Fate's juſt Laws ye muſt ſubmit,
  Nor ye, alone, conteſt
That pow'r which every Son of Man
  Has hitherto confeſt.

The ADVOCATE.

A prudent Man foreseeth the Evil, and hideth him-self: But the Simple pass on, and are punished.

PROVERBS xxii. 3.

The crafty Man the Crime perceives,
   The Guilty does protect;
The Cause of just but needy Men,
   He ever does reject.

The Poor and Guiltless are oppress'd
   By Justice' vain Pretence,
And Gold, than Laws, is found to have
   A greater Influence.

The COUNSELLOR, or MAGISTRATE.

*Whofo ftoppeth his Ears at the Cry of the Poor, he
alfo fhall cry himfelf, but fhall not be heard.*

PROVERBS xxi. 13.

The Rich and Wealthy readily
   To Suiters rich give Ear,
And fcorn the poor and needy Man,
   His Pray'r refufe to hear:

But when themfelves, in the laft Hour,
   To God fhall earneft cry,
Their anxious Pray'rs he fhall reject,
   And their Requeft deny.
     3

The CURATE, or PREACHER.

Woe unto them that call Evil Good, and Good Evil;
that put Darkness for Light, and Light for Dark-
ness; that put Bitter for Sweet, and Sweet for
Bitter.

ISAIAH V. 20.

Woe to you impious Hypocrites,
  Who Evil Goodness term;
And Evil to be truly Good,
  With equal Fraud affirm:

Who Dark for Light, with Falsehood great,
  And Light for Dark embrace;
Bitter for Sweet who substitute,
  And Sweet for Bitter place.

The PRIEST.

I myself also am a mortal Man, like to all.

WISDOM vii. 1.

The holy Sacrament, behold,
  Celeſtial Gift, I bear,
The ſick Man, at the Hour of Death,
  With certain Hope to cheer.

Ev'n I myſelf am mortal too,
  And the ſame Laws obey,
And ſhall like him, when Time ſhall come,
  To Death be made a Prey.

The FRIAR MENDICANT.

*Such as sit in Darkness, and in the Shadow of Death,
being bound in Affliction and Iron.*

PSALM cvii. 10.

Some Men, the World to circumvent
  By Fraud and Falsehood try,
By feign'd Religion, Sin to hide
  From ev'ry mortal Eye:

Of Piety an ardent love
  They outwardly profess;
But inwardly they are the Sink
  Of all Voluptuousness:

But when the End shall be at Hand,
  They like Reward shall have,
And Death, by Myriads, shall mow down
  The Wicked to the Grave.

The CANONESS.

There is a Way which feemeth Right unto a Man;
but the End thereof are the Ways of Death.

PROVERBS xiv. 12.

An Apoftrophe to DEATH.

Why doft thou, pale and envious Death,
   A facred Maid affright?
Small Glory to thee can arife
   From Victories fo flight.

Go hence, let fick or aged Men
   Thy fatal Dart employ;
But let this Virgin, innocent,
   Life's Pleafures long enjoy.

Pleafure and Joy her jocund Youth
   Should ardently purfue;
The Pleafures of the Marriage-Bed
   To her gay Youth are due.

The OLD WOMAN.

Death is better than a bitter Life or continual Sickness.

ECCLESIASTICUS XXX. 17.

Long has my Life moſt irkſome been,
  Oppreſs'd with Care and Pain ;
No anxious Wiſh my Boſom fires
  Here longer to remain.

My certain Judgment does pronounce,
  Better to die than live ;
For Death to Minds worn out with Care
  Glad Peace and Reſt will give.

D

The PHYSICIAN.

Phyſician, heal thyſelf.

LUKE iv. 23.

Diſeaſes well thou underſtand'ſt,
   And cures canſt well apply,
Which to the Sick, in Time of Need,
   Will welcome Health ſupply.

But while, O dull and ſtupid Wretch,
   Thou others Fates doſt ſtay,
Thou'rt ignorant what fell Diſeaſe
   Shall hurry thee away.

The ASTROLOGER.

Knowest thou it, because thou waſt then born ? or be-
cauſe the Number of thy Days is great ?
JOB xxxviii. 21.

Thou, by contemplating a Sphere
   Which Heav'n's bright Face does ſhow,
Events which ſhall to others chance,
   Pretendeſt to foreknow.

Tell me, if thou of Fates to come
   A ſkilful Prophet art,
When to the Tomb the Hand of Death
   Shall urge thee to depart ?

Behold the Sphere, which to thy View
   My Right-Hand now does hold,
By that the Fate which thou ſhalt find
   May better be foretold.

The MISER.

*Thou Fool, this Night thy Soul ſhall be required of
thee: Then whoſe ſhall thoſe things be which thou
haſt provided?*

LUKE xii. 20.

This Night ſhall Death, with Iron Hand,
   Thee, griping Wretch, ſubdue;
And in the narrow Grave entomb'd,
   To-Morrow thee ſhall view.

Therefore, when thou, of Life depriv'd,
   Shalt far from hence be gone,
What Succeſſor ſhall thy vaſt Heaps
   Of endleſs Riches own?

The MERCHANT.

*The getting of Treafures by a lying Tongue, is a
Vanity toffed to and fro of them that feek Death.*

PROVERBS xxi. 6.

A foolifh Part he fure purfues,
  Who Wealth by Fraud and Lies
T' accumulate, and num'rous Goods
  To gain unjuftly trics.

For Death entangled in the Snare,
  To feize him fhall not fail;
And thefe his Actions moft unjuft
  Shall caufe him to bewail.

D 3

The SHIPWRECK.

But they that will be rich, fall into Temptation, and
a Snare, and into many foolish and hurtful Lusts,
which drown Men in Destruction and Perdition.

1 TIMOTHY vi. 9.

That worldly Goods they may procure,
    And Wealth immense obtain,
Their Breasts Men hourly will expose,
    Temptations to sustain.

But Men whom Dangers thus surround,
    Fortune compels to bend
Their Footsteps to those beaten Paths
    Which to Destruction tend.

The KNIGHT, or SOLDIER.

In a Moment ſhall they die, and the People ſhall be troubled at Midnight, and paſs away: And the Mighty ſhall be taken away without Hand.

JOB xxxiv. 20.

Againſt the Man who Wars excites,
   And does mild Peace deſpiſe,
(Peace, that to all great Bleſſings brings)
   The People ſhall ariſe :

To Courage only they ſhall truſt,
   This Tyrant fierce to tame ;
And fall he ſhall, but by a Stroke
   No human Hand ſhall aim ;

For him who, to oppreſs Mankind,
   Shall mighty Arms employ,
Reſitleſs Death ſhall ſuddenly
   By an ill Fate deſtroy.

The COUNT.

For when he dieth, he fhall carry nothing away: His Glory fhall not defcend after him.

Psalm xlix. 17.

None of thofe Honours which the Great
    And Mighty now attend,
When Death fhall caft them from their Seat,
    Shall to the Grave defcend.

No Enfigns of a glorious Race
    They thither fhall convey,
Nor Titles high; for in the Grave
    They nought but Duft fhall be.

The OLD MAN.

My Breath is corrupt, my Days are extinct, the Graves are ready for me.

JOB xvii. 1.

Exhaufted Strength my feeble Nerves
   No longer now does brace,
And, like a River's rapid Stream,
   My Life flows out apace.

The Time, which no One can recall,
   How fwift a Flight has ta'en !
And nothing but the filent Tomb
   For me does now remain.

Tir'd of the Ills of a long Life,
   And fick of all its Cares,
For fpeedy Death I now addrefs
   To Heav'n my anxious Pray'rs.

The COUNTESS.

They spend their Days in Wealth, and in a Moment
go down to the Grave.

JOB xxi. 13.

In num'rous Joys their rapid Life
   The thoughtlefs Virgins wafte,
And ev'ry Kind of Pleafure feek
   With Eagernefs to tafte.

From Cares and Sorrow they are free,
   No Thought their Minds to tire,
A vacant Life, full fraught with Blifs,
   They earneftly defire.

But in the Grave they fhall be laid,
   By Death's all-piercing Dart,
Where he their Pleafures exquifite
   Shall into Grief convert.

The NEW-MARRIED COUPLE.

The Lord do so to me, and more also, if ought but
Death part thee and me.

·RUTH i. 17.

This is true Love, and this alone,
　Which Two in One conjoins,
And in Affection's ſtrongeſt Bands
　And mutual Friendſhip binds.

This Union ſhall, alas! endure
　By much too ſhort a Time;
One Death ſevere can two divide
　Whom Bands of Wedlock join.

The DUTCHESS.

Thou shalt not come down off that Bed on which thou
art gone up, but shalt surely die.

2 KINGS i. 16.

From the soft Bed, O youthful Maid,
   Whereon thy Limbs now lie,
Permission ever to arise,
   The cruel Fates deny:

For first shall Death thy lifeless Limbs
   Subdue without Remorse,
And his fell Scythe shall to the Grave
   Consign thy breathless Corse.

3

The PORTER.

Come unto me all ye that labour, and are heavy laden,
and I will give you Reſt.

MATTHEW xi, 28.

Hither advance, ye weary Throng,
  And quick my Steps attend,
Who under Loads of ſo great Weight,
  With weary Shoulders bend.

Traffic and Gain your anxious Thoughts
  Did long enough poſſeſs,
Your Breaſts the Cares which theſe produce
  No longer ſhall diſtreſs.

E

The PEASANT.

In the Sweat of thy Face shalt thou eat Bread.

GENESIS iii. 19.

Bread for thyself, by Labour great,
    Thou shalt thyself obtain ;
And from the Ground, without great Toil,
    No Suftenance shalt gain.

After long Ufe of Things below,
    And num'rous Labours paft,
Pale Death to all thy Cares and Toils
    Shall put an End at laft.

The CHILD.

Man that is born of a Woman, is of few Days, and
full of Trouble. He cometh forth like a Flower,
and is cut down: He fleeth also as a Shadow, and
continueth not.

JOB xiv. 1.

Man, who conceiv'd in the dark Womb,
   Into the World is brought,
Is born to Times with Mifery,
   And various Evil fraught.

And as the Flow'r foon fades and dies,
   However fair it be,
So finks he alfo to the Grave,
   And like a Shade does flee.

The SWISS SOLDIER.

When a strong Man armed keepeth his Palace, his Goods are in Peace. But when a stronger than he shall come upon him, and overcome him, he taketh from him all his Armour wherein he trusted, and divideth his Spoils.

LUKE xi. 21, 22.

Undaunted and secure in Arms,
　　While Strength and Life remain,
The brave his Mansions, and his Wealth
　　In Safety shall maintain.

But Death with greater Force shall wage
　　Against him War ere long,
And, for the Grave, shall cause him quit
　　His Post, no longer strong.

The GAMESTERS.

For what is a Man profited, if he shall gain the whole World, and lose his own Soul?

MATTHEW xvi. 26.

If the destructive Art of Dice
 Could Wealth immense insure,
Or Man the World by Dice could gain,
 What Good would it procure?

His Soul this Practice will destroy,
 Entangled in its Snare,
A Loss which no Art, Fraud, or Chance,
 Is able to repair.

E 3

The DRUNKARDS.

And be not drunk with Wine, wherein is Excess.

EPHESIANS V. 18.

With Wine's Excess your Souls to drench,
  Ye mortal Throng, forbear;
For Luxury of every Kind,
  And raging Lust is there.

Lest Death assail you unprepar'd,
  Oppress'd with Sleep and Wine,
And, in a Vomit foul, your Souls
  Compel you to resign.

The FOOL.

He goeth after her as an Ox goeth to the Slaughter,
or as a Fool to the Correction of the Stocks.

PROVERBS vii. 22.

No Life ſo ſweet as to be mad,
   And no one Thing to know ;
But this is far remov'd from beſt,
   As Mad-men's Actions ſhew.

Secure of Fate the witleſs Fool
   Like ſportive Lambkins treads,
And knows not that his ev'ry Step
   To Death's ſad Portals leads.

The THIEF.

O Lord, I am oppreſſed, undertake for me.

ISAIAH xxxviii. 14.

Men to deſtroy with fell Intent,
  The Thief by Night does riſe ;
But now to ſpoil an aged Dame
  Of a full Baſket tries.

I ſuffer Wrong, ſhe cries, and God
  Sends Death to her Relief,
Who, by the Hangman's certain Gripe,
  Strangles the greedy Thief.

The BLIND MAN.

*If the Blind lead the Blind, both shall fall into the
Ditch.*

MATTHEW XV. 14.

The blind Man to a Guide as blind
   Himself does here commit;
Both wanting Sight, they here descend
   Into the fatal Pit.

For, while the Man does vainly hope
   Success his Steps attends,
Into the Darkness of the Grave
   He suddenly descends.

The CHARIOTEER.

And he funk down in his Chariot.

2 KINGS ix. 24.

The Charioteer, by Horſes fierce,
   Is rapid whirl'd along;
The Reins they ſcorn, while Fear of Death
   Contends with Reaſon ſtrong.

The rapid Wheel at length torn off,
   The Axle overthrows;
While, from the Caſks, the precious Wine
   In copious Torrents flows.

The BEGGAR.

O wretched Man that I am, who shall deliver me from the Body of this Death?

ROMANS vii. 24.

He that from hence to be releas'd,
　　With Chriſt to live, deſires,
Deſpiſes Death, and to the Stars
　　In Words like theſe aſpires:

Who from this mortal Body will
　　Me wretched Man releaſe;
And ſnatch me Wretch! from this vile World,
　　To Realms of pureſt Peace?

The HUSBAND.

What taketh away the Life? Even Death.
ECCLESIASTICUS XXXi. 27*.

Remember that Death will not be long in coming.
ECCLESIASTICUS XiV. 12.

The Tyrant Death, O Husband fond,
  The worst of all its Foes,
Is to our Life and its short Course,
  With constant Steps pursues.

Reflect then in thy Prime of Life
  (Life's transitory Day)
That to thy End it thee conducts
  By gradual Decay.

   * The Original of this Passage has no corresponding Words
in the Translation of the Bible now in Use, and the above is
therefore inserted from the former Translation.

The WIFE.

Of the Woman came the Beginning of Sin, and through her we all die.

ECCLESIASTICUS XXV. 4.

From Eve, the Mother of Mankind,
   Our Parent Adam's Wife,
Sprang Sin, and thence fell Death arose,
   The Enemy of Life.

Let not, howe'er, thy tender Mind
   To Grief a Victim fall,
If Death should thee to quit this World,
   Like other Mortals, call.

F

The LAST JUDGMENT.

We shall all stand before the Judgment-Seat of Christ.
ROMANS xiv. 10.

Watch therefore, for ye know not what Hour your Lord doth come.
MATTHEW xxiv. 42.

For all his Actions to account,
   By God's exprefs Command,
Each Man before the Judgment-Seat
   Of the juft Judge fhall ftand.

Let us be therefore vigilant,
   Left, when that Time fhall come,
God, for our Actions, fhould pronounce
   A juft but angry Doom.

And fince when that Hour fhall arrive,
   No Mortal can declare;
For its Approach the pious Man
   Will watch and well prepare.

Whatsoever thou takest in Hand, remember the End,
and thou shalt never do amiss.

ECCLESIASTICUS vii. 36.

Spotless to live if thou desir'st,
   And free from every Vice,
Let this Memorial constantly
   Be placed before thine Eyes.

For it will often thee remind,
   That Death will soon arrive,
And frequent Thought to all thy Acts
   Will a due Caution give.

Vouchsafe, O Christ, with Heart sincere,
   That we thy Paths may tread,
And that to all the heav'nly Path
   May thus be open made.

*As by one Man Sin entered into the World,
and Death by Sin; and so Death passed upon
all Men, for that all have sinned.*

ROMANS V. 12.

F I N I S.

www.ingramcontent.com/pod-product-compliance
Lightning Source LLC
Chambersburg PA
CBHW032355020726
47499CB00008B/2760